Books from McNeil & Richards

Family
Love in the Caves
Three Cat Tales
Christmas Village

Humor
We're Having a Heat Wave
Brains

Suspense
The Perfect Candidate
The Anchor War
Stealing the White House
The Spy Book

Nonfiction
3D in Print

LOVE IN THE CAVES

JACK GILHOOLY

McNeil & Richards

Published by McNeil & Richards
www.mcneilandrichards.com

ISBN 13   978-0-9825602-2-8
ISBN   0982560222

for Jane

A Few Words About This Book

The following material is based on writings discovered on stone slabs, cave walls and old beer cans outside Bethlehem, Pennsylvania, the cradle of a strange civilization. The time of the writings has been pinpointed between 250,000 years and 2,000 years before Christ. Eastern Standard Time. It should be pointed out the beer cans did not date back that far; they were left by careless young archaeologists, who also smeared some of the stone slabs and cave walls with food stains. The accurate interpretation of these items may be affected beyond repair, but we'll give it a shot anyway. The thoughts and comments have been translated into something resembling English.

1

A Long Time Ago

On a scale of one to ten, weather in the old days rated about a minus eight. In winter, snow piled up high above the caves where people lived. People did not know it was snow, or where it came from, and that made it worse. Red Eyes, one of the cavepeople in the settlement near Bethlehem, Pennsylvania known as Utter Bliss, dug out of the family cave one morning and noticed everything was covered with white again. "What in the world is this stuff?' he asked. "Every year it falls on us, like taxes. Are the gods angry with us?" It was not until years later that I Think, Red Eyes' son, named it snow and said that it was the same color as clouds because snow was actually fallen clouds. Obviously the poles holding up the clouds had collapsed.

In the spring, the snow melted and rain fell. Not little showers, but torrential down-pours which gushed out of the heavens and flooded the area.

Then, the warmth of summer would dry the land and nature was in its glory. To cave-men, it was the bonkball season. They would take vacations and sleep outdoors.

In autumn, leaves on the trees would turn colors, days became cooler and the men went on hunting expeditions to find enough food to last through the winter. Storytellers would begin a new season of storytelling and let the old reruns die.

Then winter would arrive and the cycle would start again. And so it was for I Think and his family and friends.

One chilly autumn evening Red Eyes stag-gered home from the swamp where he had overindulged in berry juice with friends and he asked his wife, I Dunno, if she wanted to have a child. "I Dunno," she said, and the next year—after a cold, long winter—I Think was born.

The science of name selection was still in its infancy. Children did not have names at birth, but a year or two later they would be given names. People would ask "How's the kid?" or "How's your son?" I Dunno would say, "I dunno," but Red Eyes would say, "He's gonna make a great little caveman." They considered calling him Great Little Caveman.

I Think's first words were "I Think" and, like many other children, his name came from his first words. This was also true of his mother, I Dunno. In other cases, names were the result of a trait or characteristic others saw in the person, as it had been for I Think's father, Red Eves, who drank too much; the teacher known as Old Ironsides; and the student called Puzzled.

I Think was an unusual child. When other cavechildren roamed through the countryside pestering little animals, I Think would sit around thinking. I Dunno tried to break him of the habit but did not succeed.

When I Think was a few years older, other children allowed him to play bonkball with them, but they put him in right field and forgot about him. They told I Think he was too skinny and too short to be a good athlete. "What do you expect?" I Think asked. "I'm only eleven years old. You don't get Willie Mays for the salaries you are paying." (This could be a latter-day forgery.)

Among I Think's friends were Let Go, an appealing girl who had to fight the boys off; Foul Play, the school bully; Hug Me, an affectionate and well-mannered girl; Didja Hear, a boy who was always telling funny stories that began "Didja hear the one about ..."; Listener, a quiet boy who was known as a good listener; and Fast Talkin', a caveboy who fancied himself as a ladies' man.

2

Teenage Years

When I Think was thirteen years old, he ventured out on a double date with Fast Talkin'.

Let Go and Fast Talkin' were smooching when I Think still was trying to figure out what to say to his date, Hug Me.

"You think a lot, don't you," Hug Me noted.

"Yes."

"What do you think about?"

"Getting out of jams like this."

The girl giggled. "You are kind of cute."

"Hug Me..."

"All right."

I Think was going to say something to

her, but Hug Me moved closer and he hugged her. Courting a cavegirl was easier than I Think had expected it to be.

As the first few years of school passed, I Think felt a growing uneasiness about his education and his future. He wanted to know more. Simply counting to seven and drawing primitive artwork on cave walls did not seem fulfilling. He could talk to the more intelligent members of the small cave community, but that wouldn't take years, that would take an afternoon, and there was still so much more to know. He often asked Red Eyes questions, like "why are there stars in the sky?"

"To give us light at night when the sun is sleeping," said Red Eyes.

"You told me that one day everything was dark in the middle of the day. Then, everything was light again. What caused that?"

"The sun was taking a nap. Suns get tired, too."

I Think decided to think about that.

When I Think was fourteen, Red Eyes and the other fathers took him and his friends of the same age hunting for the first time. They wore togas, carried spears, ventured far from their caves, and huddled close together when animals came near. They heard wild animals, but didn't see many. Usually the animals were dead when the hunters brought them back to show the children.

I Think was told that henceforth, he would be expected to go on the hunts as long as he was in good health and not too old. Things like that made him hate the word "henceforth".

When he was seventeen, I Think decided to move out of his parents' cave and live in a cave of his own in a new development in a suburb of Utter Bliss. Didja Hear and Fast Talkin' visited him in his new home.

"How did you get your parents to agree to let you leave home?" Fast Talkin' wondered.

"I'm not sure. I think I insulted my mother's cooking and my dad's grocery."

"No wonder they didn't object," Didja Hear said. "They probably helped you pack."

But I Think did not cut the ties with his parents. He needed to earn hopeks to pay for his cave, so he agreed to help Red Eyes run his little grocery store.

3

Marrying Hug Me

It dawned on I Think, over the next few months, that he was not very good at taking care of a cave by himself. He saw himself as a thinker, an intellectual, and such mundane tasks as washing dishes and doing the laundry took too much of his time. Besides, he was lonely. He wanted a cavegirl to keep him company, and take care of him, and love him. Fast Talkin' had given him tips about dating and he thought about everything he had learned. Then, one evening, in the woods, he tried his new technique on Hug Me.

"You wanna move in with me?" I Think blurted out.

"I Think, I am not that kind of girl!" Hug Me told him.

I Think muttered to himself, "have patience, have patience."

"I mean, Hug Me, do you want to marry me?"

She pondered the question. "Do you love me?"

"Yes, I love you, Hug Me."

And she did.

"How are you going to convince my mother Stone Heart that she should let me marry you?" Hug Me asked.

"Why does your mother dislike me so much?"

"She says you think too much. A person shouldn't think so much."

"I'm glad she practices what she preaches."

"She also says you remind her of dad because he was lazy."

I Think sighed. "I don't suppose she has a fatal disease that will kill her in the next few months. I will go to see her."

"You wanted to talk to me?" Stone Heart asked.

I Think gulped. "Yes, Stone Heart. It is about Hug Me's happiness."

"You are going away!" she exclaimed. "How wonderful. Goodbye and good luck."

"I am not going away. You know, Stone Heart, some day I am going to do great things."

"Like going away?"

"No, Stone Heart. By thinking. By solving problems which plague us."

"Problems like you?"

"You aren't making this easy, Stone Heart. I'm talking about problems like how to ease the pain in your side, how to make you happier, how to build a better cave."

"Hmm. Tell me more, I Think."

"I will spend my life solving problems like these. Everyone will benefit."

"You've got an angle, I Think. There's something about this you aren't telling me."

"I want to marry your daughter."

"You want to marry Hug Me? You aren't good enough for Hug Me."

"Please, no compliments. Hug Me and I love each other."

"Hug Me and you? I don't think so. Hug Me should marry Tycoon. He is going to make a lot of money in his lifetime."

"Tycoon wants to marry Hold Me Tight. He is not interested in Hug Me."

"Well, I suppose Hug Me could do worse than marrying you ..."

"Thank you, Stone Heart."

"... but I'm not sure how."

Hug Me and I Think were married one autumn day with about thirty cavepeople looking on. Then the couple honeymooned briefly in Pittsburgh before returning home to their new cave.

4

The First Saloon

After a month of marriage, I Think and
Hug Me had their first fight. Hug Me said
I Think was looking at Let Go and thinking he wanted to go home with her. I Think
said he wasn't, adding "but even if I was, you
can't convict a caveman for what he's thinking."

Hug Me cried. I Think said he loved
Hug Me, but she would not talk to him. As
I Think stomped out of the cave, he acci-
dentally broke the platter Stone Heart had
given them as a wedding present. Hug Me,
of course, would not believe it had been an
accident.

"You hate my mother!" she screamed.

"Hate is a strong word," I Think said. "Maybe something like 'dislike' or 'detest' would be better."

Then Hug Me started sobbing again and I Think headed back to the old neighborhood he had grown up in. The sight of the old caves brought back memories of a happy, uncomplicated childhood. One cave I Think did not recognize, however. Chiseled on a stone in front of it were the words "Listener's Saloon". I Think entered and saw his childhood friend, Listener, at the end of a long, wooden counter.

"Well, if it isn't the honeymooner," Listener said. "How is married life?"

I Think seated himself on one of the stones in front of the counter. "Before I was married I was happy and I had an apartment. Now there's a woman in the apartment who probably won't let me in tonight and I am miserable."

"That's tough," Listener said.

"What is this place anyway?"

"It's a bar — a saloon. The world's first. We serve booze here. Fermented berries, intoxicating beverages, that sort of thing. I invented the saloon for guys with problems. Cavemen like you. What will you have?"

"Milk."

"Milk? Do you see any cows in here? I don't think you get the idea, pal. This is a saloon where I serve alcoholic beverages."

"I gave up drinking alcoholic beverages," I Think said.

"So what are you doing in my saloon?"

"I didn't know what a saloon was. That's my *second* mistake of the evening."

Listener, a patient man by nature, decided to keep the peace. "Look, I Think, let's not get angry. I don't have milk. What would you like?"

"An Italian stinger," I Think said, off the top of his head.

"An Italian stinger? What is an Italian stinger?" (This could have been a forgery—a latter-day booze bottle left in the rubble around the caves.)

"All right," I Think said. "I aim to please. Give me a Singapore sling."

"What is a Singapore sling?"

"Well, do you have Irish coffee?"

"I am trying to be patient, I Think. Quit fooling around and order."

"And you call yourself a bartender," I Think mumbled.

"Good idea. I'll call myself a bartender. So what will you have?"

"Berry beer."

"That's more like it. Now I know what you are talking about. So Hug Me threw you out, eh?"

"No, I walked out."

"Same thing. She's got the cave and you are sitting here telling me your troubles. Did you try to be reasonable? Did you try to see her side of it?"

"It started when she tried to tell me what *I* was thinking."

"Oh, yes. They are good at that. Every female thinks she can tell what you are thinking. They all think they are psychic. I wonder, I Think—did the minister say 'till death do you part' or 'till hunting season do you part'?"

"No loopholes. It was till death. Or insanity. Whichever comes first."

"Do you have a job?" Listener asked.

"I'm helping my dad in his store, but I want to be a thinker. An intellectual. Think about big problems."

"Is there money in that?"

"Probably not. I may be working in dad's store till the end of time. Between that and fighting with Hug Me, I could be spending a lot of time here. You got an extra bunk in the back?"

"No. Go home, I Think. This is a saloon, not a hotel."

"I see a bright future for saloons," I Think said.

"Me, too. That'll be five hopeks."

When I Think arrived home, Hug Me had stopped crying but she was not happy. "Well, what do you want?" she asked her hubby.

"Remember me? The clothes over in that closet belong to me. I here live."

"You here live?"

"I mean I live here."

"What's the matter with you?"

"I stopped by Listener's Saloon."

"What is a saloon?"

"An establishment run by a counselor for the health and happiness of his friends."

"You mean they sell booze."

"Do they ever." I Think put an arm around Hug Me. He kept the other one free so he could defend himself if she tried to slug him. "You know, we shouldn't have gotten mad at each other."

"I know."

"I didn't break your mother's gift intentionally. Why, I'm almost getting to the point where I can tolerate her."

"That's nice."

"Let's go to bed."

Later, I Think wrote about it in his diary. The fight started because Hug Me was telling him what *he* was thinking. It ended with him saying he was sorry. What fools we mortals be, wrote I Think.

5

The First Fast Food Restaurant

Working in Red Eyes' little grocery store did not excite I Think. He looked on it as a dead-end job. But he attempted to make the best of a bad situation. Red Eyes was struggling to pay his bills and I Think tried to help him.

"Your grocery isn't big enough," I Think said. "It isn't exciting enough to bring in more business."

"Right. So, even though I can't pay my bills, I should expand, and go further into debt. You've got a lot to learn about business, I Think."

"You've got to dream, dad. If you don't want to expand your grocery, you could try something different. If you don't get more hopeks coming in, your little grocery may not survive."

"What do you suggest, Mr. Big Shot I Think?"

"The only restaurant in Utter Bliss is at the Hotel Tycoon. It is overpriced and customers must wait forever to get their food. Start a new kind of restaurant, where the food is cheap and people get their food fast."

"I've never run a restaurant. I run a grocery."

"I know dad, but we're thinking big. It would be the first fast food restaurant ever! You could even have a drive-through for people on horses."

"I have no idea what you are talking about."

"You could call it Red Eyes' Burgers. Or McRedEyes."

"You are out of your mind. Does your mother know you are doing drugs?"

"I'm not, dad. This is me talking!"

"Good grief. Where did we go wrong?"

"I am not a therapist. That would take years to investigate."

"Smart alec kid. Get back to mopping the floors."

The next year Movin' On opened the first fast food restaurant. It was called Fast Grub. And it was located across the street from the Red Eyes Grocery.

Red Eyes stood in the doorway to his store gazing at Fast Grub. It was crowded with people.

"They are doing a lot of business," I Think noted. "You still think a fast food restaurant was a bad idea?"

"It will never last."

"The sign says they've already sold five hundred burgers."

"It will never last."

"Maybe you are right." I Think said. "We should be ready for the crowds of people who will come to our store when they go out of business."

"Smart alec kid. Mop the floors!"

6

The First Academy

I Think became increasingly frustrated working in Red Eyes' little store. He had big dreams, and wanted to accomplish much more. He intended to do important things. And if he made enough money, he could give some to Red Eyes so he could keep his store open.

I Think was not sure where to start, or how to get the money to do it. Since Tycoon was very good at making money (and owned half the real estate in the community), I Think went to see him.

"Hello, Tycoon. Long time no see."

"Oh, it's you, I Think. Sorry I couldn't

go to your wedding. I was too busy making money."

"You mean earning money?"

"No. I mean making it. I make it, since we don't have a mint."

"There must be a lot of money in that."

"There sure is. ... What do you want? I'm wasting time talking to you."

"I need advice, Tycoon. Advice about a career for someone who likes to think, like me."

"I charge five hopeks an hour for advice."

I Think followed Tycoon into his office.

"A job for an intellectual type," Tycoon muttered. "There must be something intellectuals can do that's profitable. How about serving as a government consultant?"

"I don't want to be associated with Emperor Big Feet's government," I Think declared. "I have certain principles, certain ethics ..."

"Where would I be if I had principles and ethics? I'd be broke, that's where. You've got to be more flexible in your thinking. ... Do you have any rich relatives you don't particularly like and wouldn't mind knocking off?"

"Tycoon! Don't even joke about that."

"Well, I'll think about your problem. This could be a tough one. That will be five hopeks."

Other cavepeople would see I Think meditating (or goofing off) and they would come to him for advice. He was known as the most intellectual member of the cave community. He also was the poorest member.

I Think was sitting under a tree in Utter Bliss Park when a teenage girl, Bare Ass, and several other cavechildren came over. "I have a problem, I Think," Bare Ass said. "Why does my boyfriend, Hungry Eye, always have sex on the mind?"

"He probably can't count to seven," I Think suggested.

"Should doctors be given special schooling?" April Moon asked.

"Definitely," said I Think. "One year to study medicine and three years to improve their bonkball."

"Do we have a democracy or a republic?" Hungry Eye asked.

"Under Emperor Big Feet, I would say we have an empire with shadings of totalitarianism."

Everyone oohed and ahhed and praised I Think as a smart young man.

I Think realized people in the cave community wanted to know more and had difficulty finding answers to their questions. He had an idea. He would start an academy. By paying two hopeks a week, anyone could attend his academy and benefit from his knowledge.

He posted a few signs around Utter Bliss and told friends about his new venture. Word about the academy quickly spread throughout Utter Bliss and surrounding communities.

On the first day of the academy—in early summer—ten people showed up. Two men, three women, two boys, and three girls.

"Welcome to the I Think Academy," I Think said. "During our discussions, we will talk about important things, such as poverty, the gods, Emperor Big Feet, the weather, and taxes. You will learn a great deal, I hope, and I will learn from you.

"We will begin by talking about the gods. Let's start with the Sun God. He must be kept happy or he goes away for a while, and clouds and bad weather always follow. Have you noticed that?"

They all said they had.

"How can the Sun God be kept happy?" Bare Ass asked.

"For one thing, he doesn't like all those jokes about him that have been going around. You know, like 'why does the Sun God hide every night?' 'Because he doesn't want anyone to see his pajamas.' Cheap shots like that anger the Sun God.'

A dark cloud moved overhead.

"What about the War God?" Gray Hair, the oldest of them all, asked.

"The War God does not need to be appeased every week," I Think noted. "Thank goodness. He merely wants a good little war every once in a while to keep him happy. The

War God is a rival of the Love God and they vie to see who has the most influence over us. The Love God started the saying 'make love, not war.' The War God started the sayings 'the way to peace is through war', 'the best defense is a strong offense' and 'my God, George, what happened to you?' "

"Who is George?" asked Gray Hair.

"It's a name," I Think said. "Just a name."

"Sure is a strange name," Gray Hair noted.

"Let's talk about the Love God," I Think suggested. "The Love God must not be trifled with. Either a person is in love, or the person is not in love. Never try to fool the Love God. She can be very temperamental."

One day, a few weeks later, Gray Hair asked, "What is Truth?"

"Gray Hair is asking silly questions again," commented Hungry Eye.

"It is not a silly question," I Think asserted. "The difference between us and uncivilized cavepeople are principles, such as Truth, Honor, Justice, Equality. What is Truth? The answer is not as simple as you would think. Truth is something that is in agreement with reality. It is a fact. It is true. But what was Truth yesterday might be a lie today."

Bare Ass nodded. "Like when Red Eyes says he has no bananas in his grocery. Today, that could be true. Tomorrow, he could receive a shipment of bananas and it would not be true."

"Very good, Bare Ass."

"And what about Equality?" Didja Hear said. "I believe no one in our society should be more equal than others. No one should have special advantages. Everyone should have a right to speak out and a right to vote."

Such comments made I Think nervous. If Emperor Big Feet got wind of them, he might shut down the academy. I Think closed the door to the cave in case any of the emperor's spies happened to pass by.

"In our settlement, everyone has an equal right to remain silent," noted Hungry Eye.

7

Inventing the Wheel and the Chariot

One day I Think and his students took off on a field trip to Utter Chaos. They came across a fallen tree in the woods. I Think looked at it and told his students to cut two slices off the tree trunk, about two inches thick. The slices were circular. Hungry Eye rolled one of the slices over to Nice Smile, a new girl in the academy.

"You couldn't do that easily if it was square, but since it is circular, it rolls along smoothly," I Think pointed out. "Let's take these two pieces of wood back to the academy with us and see what we can do with them."

The next day, when the group reported to I Think's cave for class, I Think announced, "we are going to begin a new project." He held up one of the slices of tree trunk. "I cut a hole out of the middle of this tree slice, but the hole didn't go all the way through it. Then I put a pole into the hole in the wheel and made sure it was a tight fit. Then I connected the pole to a hole in another tree slice, so we have circular wheels on each end of the pole."

"Yesterday they were part of a tree," Nice Smile pointed out.

"Yes, but now they are wheels because they are connected by a pole and the wheels can turn. Like this. Now, suppose we take a flat piece of wood and place a chair on the piece of wood and attach the chair to the platform. Then we will attach the pole to the bottom of the platform, so there is now a chair on a platform and a wheel on each side of the platform. What will we have?"

"A chair sitting on two wheels," Puzzled replied.

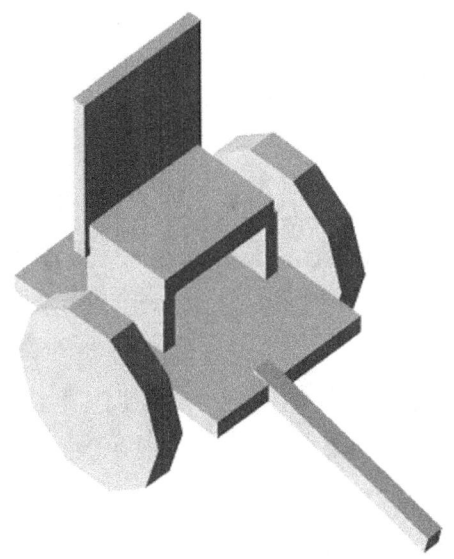

"Yes, but what does this mean?"

"There you have me," Puzzled said.

"It would be a little vehicle. A means of transportation."

Puzzled considered that. "You mean you could pull somebody in it?"

"Or you could put your belongings in the chair and pull it. It would take much less effort than if you were carrying them."

"I don't think it will work," Pessimist said.

"We should try!" I Think insisted. "This could be a great discovery!"

"Doubt it," said Pessimist.

As the class put together the vehicle, Bright Eyes said, "we could have an animal pull the vehicle. It would take us from place to place!"

"That's good thinking," I Think said.

I Think hooked a cow up to the new vehicle. The cow didn't know what to do. Then he tried a pig. No luck. I Think was beginning to think the new project might need to be abandoned. "Well, let's try that horse over there."

I Think and the students hooked the horse up to the cart. I Think climbed up on the chair.

"Let's go, Midnight! C'mon babe, let's go!"

Midnight took off and for the first time humans were able to take a ride in a vehicle instead of on top of an animal.

"I'm going to call it a chariot," I Think

declared. "You can each have a ride in the chariot, and then, in the next few days, we will make more of them."

Two weeks later, when Tycoon noticed chariots scattered around Utter Bliss, he sensed that he could sell chariots for a profit. He opened a new business, Tycoon's Chariot Company. Soon, people were using them for transportation and for racing. Tycoon manufactured them, sold them for five hopeks and gave the academy one hopek for each chariot he sold.

8

Becoming a Father

A little more than a year after her marriage to I Think, Hug Me gave birth to a son. At first the child did not have a name, of course, and everyone would ask "How's the kid?" or "How's your son?" Red Eyes, who now was a proud grandfather, would say, "He's gonna make a great little caveman." Hug Me suggested they name their son after I Think, and I Think didn't put up much of an argument. So it was agreed. They would call the boy I Think, Too.

Hug Me loved I Think, Too and would happily take him along wherever she went. She didn't go out as often as before, however, and I Think found himself saddled with more household chores than ever. Sometimes I Think would take his students along as he folded the laundry or bought the groceries and they would discuss important topics, such as whether there was a Laundry God and why food prices often went up but never went down.

Two years after I Think, Too was born Hug Me gave birth to another child. I Think and Hug Me thought about what to name the little girl and finally decided to name it Hug Me, Too.

And three years after that, Hug Me gave birth to a third child. She asked I Think what he wanted to name the kid. "How about That's Enough," he suggested.

But they named the boy Great Little Caveman.

9

Writing a Book

Hug Me told I Think they needed a bigger cave to live in. He went to see Tycoon, who handled all real estate transactions. "It's going to be expensive," Tycoon said. "You'll need some hopeks."

I Think said he didn't have enough hopeks, since he had to feed the wife and kids and pay his utility bills.

"You could earn some hopeks," Tycoon suggested. "Why don't you write some books? Write about things that will interest people. How about *What Every Cavegirl Should Know*. Or *Sex and the Single Caveman*. Or *Rape in the Academy*!"

"Good grief," said I Think. "What would later civilizations think if they found stone slabs covered with scribblings about *Rape in the Academy*? What kind of academy do you think I'm running?"

"I don't know. There have been a lot of rumors."

"I must write more serious books, like *An Introduction to Philosophy* or *Brave Old World*."

"Suit yourself," Tycoon said. "I will be your agent. That means I will get ten percent of the money. And I will be your publisher, so I'll get most of the rest of your money."

I Think temporarily discontinued classes at his academy so he could write a book. He would sit under a tree, doing nothing but thinking about what he would write.

"Help me with the laundry," said Hug Me.

"I can't," I Think insisted. "I'm busy planning my book."

"You are just goofing off again."

"No, writing a book is tough work. You

would understand if you had written a
book."

"I'll trade you. You do the laundry and
I'll sit under the tree."

"You don't understand the artistic tem-
perament."

"I don't even know what 'artistic temper-
ament' is,"

"Proves my point," I Think declared,
ending the conversation.

The problem of what to write about was
solved when the academy decided to embark
on a new project: writing down some of the
community's oral literature—stories which
had been passed down from generation to
generation. In this way, they reasoned, the
stories would not be lost to future generations and they would not change so much
with retelling.

"You know how it is," I Think told the students. "One person tells a story to another,
then that person tells the story to other
people, and before you know it, the facts
are blown out of proportion. Soon, people

are saying things like 'our ancestors were forty feet tall and they beat up dinosaurs for fun'."

Hungry Eye nodded. "That was my grandfather, Evil Eye. He could start fires by rubbing two trees together."

10

Story No. 1 from Stories Cavepeople Told—

Is There Life After Pittsburgh?

Long ago, in a strange and distant land known as Pittsburgh, there lived a giant brontosaurus named Doomsday. The cavepeople called him that because whenever the brontosaurus chased after cavepeople, they knew the end was near for one of them. They prayed Doomsday would leave them alone, because they figured it would take a real heathen creature to mangle a mortal when he was praying to the swamp god, but unfortunately for them, this brontosaurus was a real heathen creature. (It should be noted that the population of Pittsburgh was one in those days. The cavepeople left the city to Doomsday and moved to the suburbs.)

Doomsday had a big appetite. He would devour cows, horses. pigs, many gallons of swamp water ... and on special occasions, such as holidays and Sundays, he would dine in the suburbs and devour a human.

The cavepeople weren't too crazy about Doomsday's eating habits and decided something had to be done before the situation got out of hand. They decided the brontosaurus must be killed to keep their community safe.

"Who will do it?" Chicken Heart, one of the elders of the cave community, asked.

"Well, I would like to help you out," Faint Heart, Chicken Heart's son, said, "but I've got this back condition. An old bonkball injury. Some days I can hardly move."

Bad Teeth took a step backward, to make sure no one would think he was volunteering. "Actually, I've been thinking about going on a little vacation. I've been awfully tired lately."

"I'd like to help," Pale Face said, "but the little woman won't let me."

"Didn't know you were married," commented Bad Teeth.

"He's not," Faint Heart pointed out. "The little woman is his mother."

"What's the matter with all of you?" Chicken Heart demanded. "Is everyone in this settlement a coward?"

"We are not cowards," Bad Teeth insisted. "There is a difference between cowardice and wanting to live."

"But somebody has got to kill Doomsday!" Chicken Heart declared.

"What about you?" asked Weak Knees.

"I'd like to, but I've got this heart condition."

"That's why you should be the one to confront Doomsday!" suggested Weak Knees.

Chicken Heart ignored him.

They returned home to their caves to ponder the problem they had with their large and crude neighbor. The next week was a bed one. There was a Sunday *and* a holiday

(Mohagen's Birthday; Mohagen was one of the Founding Fathers of their community) and Doomsday wandered over twice to dine.

"I've got an idea," Chicken Heart told the others. "We could feed Doomsday some of my wife's cooking. If that doesn't kill him, it should at least cripple him."

"It won't work," Bad Teeth said. "The brontosaurus craves only humans, livestock and swamp water."

The others nodded sagely.

"We must find a solution to this problem," Chicken Heart insisted.

The cavemen returned to their caves and the next Sunday Doomsday paid them another visit.

"At least there is no population crisis," Faint Heart noted. "There's no overcrowding around here."

"At this rate, there won't be any of us left in two years," Chicken Heart complained. "If we stop celebrating holidays, we can last a little longer."

The next day, a stranger wearing a bearskin rode into town.

"Hello, cavepeople," the stranger said. "I am Good Guy. You can tell by my white horse. Tell me: is there something good and noble and kind I can do for you fine people?"

"There sure is," purred True Heart, Chicken Heart's teenage daughter.

"Business first, honey," Good Guy said.

"You arrived at just the right time," Chicken Heart said.

"Yeah," True Heart said.

Chicken Heart stepped up. "Shut up, True Heart. Mister, we've got one big problem here. Maybe you could get rid of it for us."

"What's your problem?"

"Doomsday. He's a big brontosaurus that hangs around Pittsburgh. Every few days he wanders over here and and devours our people. We don't mind him being a gourmet, but he's kind of depopulating the community. You know what I mean?

"I understand," Good Guy said. "I'll go

have a talk with him. Just point me in the right direction."

"It is over there," Faint Heart said. "Where the pollution is."

"Right. I'll see you later, nice people." Good Guy jumped on his horse. "You'd better make this a take," he joked. "We may not be able to reshoot it."

As the cavepeople watched Good Guy ride off in search of Doomsday, Chicken Heart grumbled, "What was he talking about?"

"I don't know," Faint Heart said. "He can't be completely sane if he's going after the brontosaurus."

Good Guy rode for an hour before he spotted Doomsday in a clearing ahead. He climbed down off his horse and retrieved the rope that was tied to his saddle. A few feet away was a cliff overlooking a valley. Good Guy strung the rope between two trees that were about ten feet apart, going back and forth between the trees several times. Then he climbed back on the horse and rode out toward Doomsday.

"Well, here I am big boy," Good Guy yelled. "Some of your neighbors aren't happy about your dining habits. They want me to take care of the problem for them."

The brontosaurus growled loudly.

Good Guy rode closer. "Why you slimy, ill-mannered, vile smelling monster. You've got the disposition of a mad dog."

The brontosaurus growled again.

"You couldn't catch me if you were wearing roller skates," Good Guy taunted.

The brontosaurus growled even louder.

"You see that tree over there?"

The brontosaurus looked.

"That tree is smarter than you are!"

The brontosaurus lumbered toward Good Guy. Good Guy rode to the end of the clearing, rode around to the back of the rope he had strung between the two trees, and planted himself and his horse behind the rope.

"C'mon, Slow Poke!" Good Guy yelled. "I haven't got all day."

The brontosaurus growled, moseyed up to Good Guy and lunged toward him. The rope tripped Doomsday, and Good Guy hurried out of the way as the brontosaurus plunged down the cliff and into the valley below.

Good Guy made sure the brontosaurus was dead, then hightailed it back to the suburbs.

"He won't be bothering you any more," Good Guy assured the townspeople.

"You did it!" True Heart exclaimed. "You got Doomsday!"

"You might say he took a giant leap for all mankind," Good Guy declared.

"That's great!" Chicken Heart said. "How can we repay you?"

"Oh, ten thousand hopeks will do for a start. True Heart can take care of the rest of your debt."

Chicken Heart hesitated.

"What's the matter, pop?" asked Faint Heart.

"I was wondering if we could get the brontosaurus back," Chicken Heart said.

11

Story No. 2 from Stories Cavepeople Told—

The Big Hunt

Once, in a far away land, the cavemen vowed that they would go on the most successful hunt ever. They told their wives and children they would bring back more skins of big animals and more meat than any hunters had ever brought back before. And they agreed that the hunter who bagged the most big game would be awarded one hundred hopeks.

The cavemen began their journey in early autumn, when leaves on the trees were still green. The hunting went rather slowly at first, with the hunters bagging only a few rabbits, cows, and small elephants.

They pushed on, into lush hunting lands

they had never traveled before. They confronted huge animals they had never seen before—massive dinosaurs, big and awesome birds, and wild hippos.

The hunters did not know the terrain very well, but they pressed on and continued to fill their hunting quotas.

After a month they returned home. It had been a successful hunt but one of their countrymen, Time to Go, was missing. They hoped he was merely lost and would turn up eventually.

All the cavepeople turned out for a village gathering and the hunters prepared to show them what they had brought back. Who was the greatest hunter of all? Who would win the one hundred hopek prize?

"I bagged one dinosaur, one cow, five squirrels," Little Eagle said.

"I got one dinosaur, one brontosaurus, one cow and four rabbits," Me Also proclaimed.

"That's nothing," said Sharp Eye. "I bagged one big wild bird, one dinosaur, two cows, and four rabbits."

Then everyone looked at Shy But Strong.

"I got one cow, three rabbits, one squirrel, and Time to Go."

The others stared at him. "What do you mean?" they asked. Time to Go was one of the hunters, one of their neighbors.

"Haven't you ever heard of a hunting accident?" Shy But Strong asked. "I told Time to Go there was a lion coming after him and that he should go back. Well, I didn't know there was quicksand in back of him. But it didn't matter because the lion got him before the quicksand did. So, anyway, I kind of felt responsible and I brought Time to Go's body back. Now the question is, do I count him as part of my catch?"

The others looked at Shy But Strong with growing anger. Then they ran after him, waving clubs and knives.

"Does that mean yes or no?" Shy But Strong yelled back.

12

Publishing the Book

Several months later, I Think delivered the hundred and fifty stone slabs to Tycoon in a chariot.

Tycoon hired twenty caveteenagers to make copies. A month later, he had twenty copies of the book ready to sell. I Think put up signs around Bethlehem and Utter Bliss advertising *Stories Cavepeople Told*. He even sent a copy to Crazy Jake in Philadelphia.

Some of I Think's students and a few housewives bought the first copies. The copy I Think sent to Philadelphia came back in pieces. Obviously Crazy Jake was an anti-intellectual.

Since most of the first edition was sold out, Tycoon ordered a second edition. On the cover he added the words: "The Dynamic New Bestseller!"

Students in the academy looked on I Think with new respect. He had written a book. And they expected him to write more. That is how the "publish or perish" problem first arose in institutions of higher learning.

13

The Big War

When I Think was thirty-four years old, Bethlehem and Utter Bliss became entangled in a serious dispute with their neighbors, Philadelphia and Pittsburgh. Emperor Big Feet drafted many of his male subjects into his army as he prepared for war.

When the recruits gathered on the edge of Utter Bliss, Sergeant Follow Me read them a message from Emperor Big Feet. He said fighting seemed likely and it probably would be the biggest war in all caveman history. Unfortunately, the emperor said, he had duties to attend to at home and could not go along, but he assured them his thoughts would be with them.

Gray Hair was particularly upset to be

drafted. "What am I doing here? I am fifty-eight years old!"

"Any able-bodied male over sixteen years old is eligible to be drafted," said Follow Me.

"What do you mean able-bodied?" asked Listener. "I shouldn't be here. I'm 4-F."

"4-F?" repeated Follow Me.

"Yeah. Fat, flaky, frustrated and fed up."

"Seems like they ought to make an exception for old men," Gray Hair said. "What happens when my eyesight fails and I'm too weak to fight?"

"Then we move you up to the front lines. You'll die as a hero rather than home in bed."

"I was not meant to be a hero," Gray Hair muttered. "Let me go home. Don't you respect the wishes of a dying man?"

"You are not dying."

"I will be if you send me to the front lines."

Puzzled had a concern, too. "I'm not crazy about this idea of advancing in waves, one group after another. If we retreat, we will be killed by our own men."

"That's right," Follow Me said. "The desertion rate is kept to a minimum. Any other questions?"

"Maybe I should go to officers candidate school," Hungry Eye suggested. "Then, when I come back in two years, if there's still a war going on, I can serve you better."

"Are all of you cowards?" Follow Me growled in disgust.

"We prefer to think of us as intellectuals, questioning why you tell us to do stupid things rather than merely doing them," I Think said.

"Enough of that!" Follow Me barked. "We will have no dissension in this platoon. I will train you to be soldiers if it is the last thing I do."

"We should be so lucky," Gray Hair suggested.

The war did not last very long. Crazy Jake's Philadelphia troops invaded Bethlehem and took over a hospital. Steel Head's Pittsburgh troops invaded Utter Bliss but were turned back. Crazy Jake, who had launched the attack because he wanted more land to rule over, told his troops to give back the hospital and retreat. "It would cost us a fortune to run the thing!" he told his advisers.

Peace talks were held at the Crazy Jake Motel in Philadelphia and basically all parties to the conflict agreed to return to the boundaries they had occupied before the war.

"This is so humiliating," Crazy Jake moaned.

14

Running for Emperor

And so I Think and his pals became war veterans.

When his fortieth birthday rolled around, I Think dealt with a crisis of confidence. He visited Listener's Saloon and went on a three-day drunken binge.

"You aren't over-the-hill just because you are turning forty," Listener assured him.

"Some people burn out early. Did you see my listing in *Who's Who in the Caves*? It read, 'Think, I. Lives in Utter Bliss. Son of Red Eyes and I Dunno. Founder of I Think Academy. Author of two books. Married Hug Me. Father of three children. War veteran.'"

"What's wrong with that?" Listener said. "My entry said, 'Listener. Owns saloon in

Utter Bliss. The first bartender.' They didn't mention I was in the war. Killed four people. Do they list that? No."

"You killed four of the enemy?" I Think asked.

"Well, not exactly. I said I killed four people. I didn't get the word soon enough that the Pocono people were our allies and I mowed down four of them. How was I to know?"

"I want to accomplish more," I Think said. "I want to have more of an impact on the world. Do you understand what I'm saying?"

"Uh huh. You are power hungry."

"That sounds so crass. Let's just say I want to help people."

"Helping people is the Salvation Army thing. You want to manipulate people. That's the Emperor Big Feet thing."

"You are right. I should run for Emperor!"

"Big Feet is Emperor. He will not let you take his office away from him."

"Big Feet must listen to new ideas!"

"The only idea Big Feet will listen to is raising his salary," Listener suggested.

Nevertheless, I Think scheduled an appointment to see Big Feet.

"What do you want, I Think?"

"I wish to talk to you. You know, Big Feet, you really are a popular, talented emperor."

"Lord, it's getting deep in here."

"I mean it, Big Feet. I always admired the way you keep your mind open to new ideas."

"Not me. I like the old ideas just fine. We've got a nice little settlement here."

"That's why you are so popular, Big Feet. I bet in an election, the people would elect you by a landslide."

"Who said anything about an election? And what do elections have to do with rock-slides?"

"Landslides. I meant that you would win very easily."

"Elections are for insecure rulers," Big

Feet said. "I am not insecure. I don't need to prove my popularity!"

"I don't think that's the purpose of elections," I Think said. "Elections give people the opportunity to choose whether they want to return you and your policies to office or whether they want to elect someone else as emperor."

"That's foolish. Why would an emperor agree to such a thing?"

"We don't have a constitution, so the people must rely on the innate goodness and sense of justice of the emperor."

"Yes, well, good luck with that."

"Don't you see what a great ruler you would be if you agreed to an election? You would be remembered all through history."

"All through history? For thousands of years?"

"Well, maybe not that long."

"Perhaps I will be remembered as Big Feet the Great. Doesn't sound right. You know, I never was fond of the name Big Feet. Of course, Crazy Jake in Philadelphia has it

worse. Had a terrible time at the peace con-
ference. Nearly started another war."

"That's another thing. The campaign will
give you a chance to talk about everything
you've done to—I mean, done for—our settlement. You can talk about the war, foreign
affairs ..."

"A ruler should never mess around with
women in other settlements. Politically, it's
dumb. Could start another war."

"Yes, well, you could talk about your
domestic programs and the economy."

"Maybe not talk much about the economy. A lot of people haven't forgiven me for
the inflation we had. I keep telling them it
was Tycoon's fault."

"You can brag about yourself in a campaign," I Think pointed out.

"Well, all right. I'll call an election. But
who would be dumb enough to run against
me?"

"Me," I Think muttered.

"That figures. You should have mentioned
that earlier. I would have agreed to it right
away. We will start campaign tomorrow.

Election will be in one month. We should settle on one point: Do we hang the loser?"

"No, definitely not!"

"Too bad. Seems like there ought to be more at stake. Now go away and let me take my nap."

That afternoon, I Think told his academy students he was shutting down the academy temporarily because he was running for emperor against Big Feet.

"We will help your campaign," Puzzled said. "It will be good experience for us. What should we do?"

"Pray a lot," suggested Hungry Eye.

"What are you going to campaign on?" April Moon asked.

"My feet," I Think said.

"Great," Puzzled muttered. "It will be 'my feet' against Big Feet."

"I meant, what issues are you going to campaign on?" April Moon said.

"Inflation, Big Feet's hawkish foreign policy, poverty and Big Feet's personality."

"Are we for or against poverty?" Puzzled asked.

"We are against it, of course."

The students created several posters to post on trees. Some said merely "I Think for Emperor." Puzzled's said "Give Big Feet the boot!"

I Think campaigned for change and lower taxes and against war. At his rallies, students occasionally gave him a copy of one of his books to autograph, and one cavewoman handed him a baby to autograph.

"No, I think I will kiss the baby," I Think said, and another terrible political tradition was born.

Tycoon was pissed off because Big Feet kept blaming him for inflation so Tycoon offered to start up a political slush fund for I Think. I Think declined the offer, but suggested Tycoon could use the money to fund advertising and posters supporting I Think.

Big Feet's supporters defaced posters promoting "I Think for Emperor" and they soon read "I Stink for Emperor". But I Think's supporters were capable of gutter politics, too, and Big Feet's posters soon read "Big Cheat".

I Think received a letter from Philadelphia that asked how many times Crazy Jake could vote in the election. I Think reluctantly replied that Crazy Jake was not eligible to vote in Utter Bliss' election.

During the only debate between them, I Think asked Big Feet what he would do to get rid of poverty in Utter Bliss.

 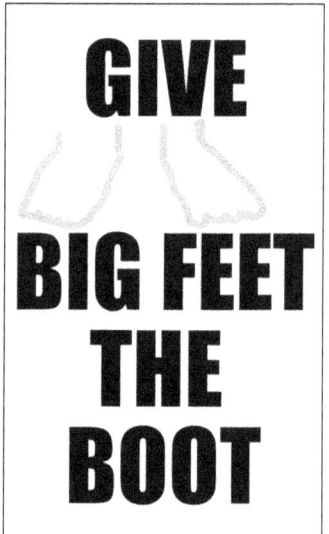

POLITICAL POSTERS

"Hmm. Well, I could send the poor to live in Philadelphia."

"But that's not getting rid of the problem."

"Actually, it is," Big Feet pointed out. "It is all I can do, because the people do not want me to raise taxes!"

A loud cheer greeted the Emperor's remarks.

On Election Day, it was evident as the first few precinct results trickled in that I Think had suffered a devastating defeat. People did not want change, and I Think lost in a rockslide. I Think delivered a concession speech to the crowd.

"The people have made their choice," he said. "A stupid choice, but they have spoken. I wish Emperor Big Feet good luck. I thought that his emotional speech about his cow, Checkers, was a bit much, but I suppose he ran an effective campaign. I want to thank those who supported my campaign and point out that if you had worked harder we might have won. But that is sour grapes. Our people should insist that elections be held on a regular basis to ensure that our rulers are held accountable for their actions. Well, at the very least this was an experience we will not forget. However we may try."

15

After the Last Hurrah

After the election, I Think was terribly depressed. He did not return to his academy immediately. He needed time for his wounds to heal.

He wandered into the woods to think and avoided cavepeople who wanted to talk about his campaign. He particularly hated the jokes some people made about his campaign. Good Lord, does a person joke about getting speared on a hunt, or falling off a mountain? Then why joke about I Think's disastrous political experience? Still, he knew nasty jokes were making the rounds. Jokes like "Did you hear they are going to hold the last election over again?" "No. Why?"

"I Think got twenty-three votes and he has only twenty-one relatives." Cheap shots like that.

I Think pondered things like the meaning of life, and defeat, and ingrown toenails. He considered moving to Utter Defeat, but that would solve nothing.

Big Feet had been generous in victory, but why shouldn't he be? He even suggested I Think run against him in the next election. "Any time you want, I Think. I like to run against you." That smart alec.

I Think figured he probably had set politics and democracy back a century or two.

16

Writing the First Dictionary

I Think pondered what he should do next. He wandered into the woods to think about it. April Moon spotted him sitting on a log.

"What will you do now, I Think?"

"Unless I take up bank robbery or join the mob, my options are limited. I was always good at inventing things. There must be something left to invent. This can't be all there is to life ... I don't know what to do. I'm buffaloed."

"You are not a buffalo, I Think. You don't even look like one."

"No, I mean I'm stymied, frustrated, thwarted, exasperated."

"You are so smart, I Think. You know more words than any other caveman."

"I suppose so."

"I just love to hear you talk."

"You know, April Moon, I could write down what I know about words. Define them, so everyone will know what they mean. I could write a dictionary. The first dictionary!"

"What is a dictionary?"

"It will be a book that defines words, listing them in alphabetical order. That way, if anyone wants to find the meaning or spelling of a word, she can look it up in my dictionary."

'That's wonderful, I Think. Will it have a plot?"

"No, it is not that kind of book."

"Well, maybe it will sell anyway."

I Think went home and began chiseling on piles of stone slabs. He tried to think of all the words he could. He listed the words and their meanings, then arranged the slabs in alphabetical order. He started with the easy words, like "mother" and "father" and moved on to other words which were in common usage in the settlement— words like cave, saloon, emperor, war, dinner, grocery and chariot. Then he listed words which were more abstract in meaning—words such as god, life, economy and frustration.

I Think pondered some more. There must be more than forty-three words. He thought of a few additional words, then walked around the settlement carrying a stone slab as he wrote down words he heard people using. He went to Philadelphia, where Crazy Jake ruled, and he heard a few more words. Some of them were obscene.

Then I Think began putting all the words in order and he wrote the first dictionary. He probably did not list all the words in existence, but he had made a start.

Among the entries in *I Think's Dictionary* were these:

> **Army**, *n.*, a body of men forced by an emperor or some other ruler to fight with clubs and knives. Sometimes they are forced to engage in a war.

Afoot, *n.*, one foot. Also *v.*, meaning under way. As in something amiss is afoot.

Amiss, *n.*, as good as amile.

Blonde, *n.*, a girl or woman with light colored hair. Also a poison, as in "you touch that blonde and I'll knock your lights out!"

Bonkball, *n.*, the national pastime, a sport played with a round ball. Also, one of the grounds often cited for divorce.

Chariot, *n.*, a vehicle consisting of a chair on two wheels. Invented by I Think. Also, a drink invented by Listener.

Dandelion, *n.*, the official flower of Bethlehem. Also a hunting expression, as in "he was a real dandelion, but we killed him."

Emperor, *n.*, an all-powerful ruler, sometimes possessing a small brain and big feet.

Financier, *n.*, an expert in handling hopeks and manipulating people.

Freedom, *n.*, a right, the absence of restraint. Also a punching bag of Emperor Big Feet.

Marriage, *n.*, a legalized union of a man and woman. Similar to war, only on a smaller scale.

Morning, *n.*, the name for the time between midnight and noon. Invented by the morning god. Named by I Think.

Ollady, *n.*, term often used to denote a wife or mother-in-law. Also, the sound made in yodeling.

Potted, *adj.*, referring to plants or drunken husbands.

5wamp god, *n.*, the god responsible for overseeing the swamps. Since this is a nasty job, the swamp god tends to have a cranky disposition and bad breath. He pals around with the war god.

Together, *adv.*, being at the same place at the same time; *v.*, to pick, as in "they went to the woods together berries."

War, *n.*, fighting between two or more collective, armed bodies. For example, the Great War fought by Bethlehem, Utter Bliss, Philadelphia and Pittsburgh. Also, a scheme to provide employment for generals and entertainment or ego satisfaction for rulers.

Also a *verb*: They war going to Listener's Saloon to get stewed.

Wheel, *n.*, a circular disc turning on a central axis; Also, slang when referring to chariots. "Dad, can I take the wheels tonight?" Said questioner wants the entire chariot, not just the wheels.

Wife, *n.*, marriage partner, also known as sparring partner, conscience and timekeeper. Example: "It is 6:11. It's about time you got home!"

When I Think finished his dictionary he took it over to Tycoon. Tycoon, besides taking offense at some of the entries referring to business and the economy, did not feel it would sell. However, he reluctantly agreed to have his girls make several copies of it. Soon many copies of the *I Think Dictionary* could be seen in Utter Bliss.

17

Goodbye, Hug Me

Hug Me and I Think slowed the pace of their lives as they reached their fifties and sixties. I Think could not quite understand how he had gotten to be eight years older than Hug Me. When they were children, he had been only three months older than her. I Think had the feeling Hug Me wasn't counting all the years she was supposed to. But he never said much about it because if that was what she wanted, it was all right with him. Besides, she did not look sixty. She would always be that young cavegirl he fell in love with more than forty years earlier.

I Think occasionally would take Hug Me dining at the Tycoon Towers, where they would dance and dine on dinosaur steaks. Afterwards, I Think would drive Hug Me back to the cave in their horse-drawn chariot.

"Some things never change," said Hug Me. "Look at the stars in the sky. Aren't they beautiful."

"Uh huh."

"Do you think we'll come back in another lifetime?" Hug Me asked her husband.

"Doesn't seem likely to me. All my life, I've been looking at things scientifically, asking questions, trying to find answers. Believing what I see, finding it hard to believe things I can't see."

Hug Me sighed. "I would like to believe we are going to be together again. It would be nice to live another lifetime with you."

A tear formed in I Think's eyes. "I would like to live another lifetime with you, too."

I Think hired a young woman to come in to keep the cave clean and do the laundry, but sometimes Hug Me insisted on doing the laundry herself. One cool spring day she was lugging a basket of laundry to the Lehigh River when she tripped on a log and rolled down an embankment. She fell about eight feet and felt pain. She called to one of the other women to get I Think, and I Think and Hungry Eye carried her back to the cave on a stretcher. Then Hungry Eye fetched the doctor, Pay Now.

Pay Now arrived a few minutes later. Hug Me told him what happened and said the pain was in her chest.

"Is it bad?" asked the doctor.

"It isn't good."

Pay Now examined her. "I'm not sure what I can do to help. There's so much we don't know about medicine. I can't tell exactly what the problem is, or what to do about it."

He gave Hug Me a strong herb to ease the pain. "I'll be back tomorrow. If she gets worse, call me immediately."

I Think nodded and reached for his hopeks. "How much do we owe you?"

"Nothing. If I could help, I might charge

you something, but I don't know how to help."

Pay Now left. I Think gave Hug Me another pillow and blanket and tried to make her more comfortable.

Hug Me liked having her family around her, but the pain got worse. She suffered through the night.

The next morning, Hug Me passed away. She was in pain no longer. I Think held her hand and cried. It had nearly killed him to see her in pain and not know how to help her.

"But maybe, Hug Me, I will see you again in some other life. If you say it is so, I believe it."

18

I Think in Retirement

I Think realized it could be a long time before he died and he should not entirely waste the rest of his time on earth. He became a part-time consultant to a new academy—Hungry Eye had finally started his own—and he began writing poetry. He wrote about his thoughts, Utter Bliss and his friends. He did not think it was great poetry, but there was nothing to compare it with. Soon cave walls around Utter Bliss and points north began sporting such verses as these:

THE CANVAS OF LIFE

The world is like a canvas
on which you paint your life;

stay within the boundaries,
don't rip it with your knife.
When you are done, hang it up
for all eternity to see —
it will inspire others to do
their best, just like you and me.

Some of his poetry took a subversive turn:

OUR EMPEROR
     (free verse)
O Big Feet — enemy of freedom
guardian of ignorance
possessor of our tax money
worshipper of war.
We have long forgotten
who made you emperor
but if we ever find him
there will be one less subject
for you to push around.

19

Knowing When
to Leave

When he was in his sixties, I Think visited Listener's Saloon for the last time.

"What will you have?" asked Listener, Too. He was Listener's son, and he helped his dad run the saloon.

"A banana daiquiri."

"We don't have anything like that."

"All right. A Moscow marauder."

"You must be I Think. Dad warned me about you."

Listener, Too fetched a berry beer for I Think as Listener came out from the back room.

"A banana daiquiri. You just don't give up, do you?" he told I Think.

"And you call yourself a bartender."

"How have you been, buddy?"

"I miss Hug Me. And I can't drink like I used to. The digestive system is shot."

"Sorry I asked. Didn't want a full medical report. It was just a polite question."

"A rhetorical question."

"Whatever."

As I Think sipped his berry beer, Listener said, "Things aren't like they used to be. Back then, people took time to enjoy life."

I Think nodded. "You must take time to smell the dandelions. And you can still accomplish more than young people today accomplish."

Didja Hear and Fast Talkin' entered. They, too, showed the effects of aging. Didja Hear was bald on top, and Fast Talkin's hair was gray. He no longer talked as fast as he once did.

Listener continued to reminisce. "Kids have it so easy today. When we were kids, this place was a frontier. We were tough. We lived the vigorous life."

I Think nodded. "Kids today think there was always a wheel. They think people always had chariots to ride around in. They think there were always academies and dictionaries ..."

"... and saloons."

"What's the world coming to?" Didja Hear lamented. "People are even living outside of caves now. I don't think it will last, though. Too many problems."

"Did any of your students accomplish anything worthwhile?" Listener asked I Think.

"Hungry Eye invented the wooden desk. April Moon wrote the first love story. Bare Ass was the first interior cave decorator."

"What did Puzzled invent?"

"Ulcers."

"One thing that bothers me is the generation gap," Fast Talkin' noted.

"Generation gap? Never heard of it," Listener said.

"It's the problem that arises when you are a generation older than the beautiful young cavewomen."

"It is two generations in your case," Listener noted. "I Think, do you have any regrets?"

"Yes. I was hoping to get a banana daiquiri."

"I mean about your life."

"Oh. No, I don't think so. I wish Hug Me wouldn't have suffered when she died. And I have fears about the future of humans."

"What are people supposed to do in retirement, anyway?" Fast Talkin' asked. "I'm having a hard time adjusting. They tell me I'm not supposed to chase after girls forty years younger than I am ..."

"Who tells you?" Listener asked.

"My wife, Let Go. And they tell me I'm not supposed to play as much bonkball, or run around so much. And I'm not supposed to exert myself, or go to work."

"That part should be nothing new for you," Listener suggested.

"This is a serious problem," said Fast Talkin'. "How am I supposed to act?"

"Look at it this way," I Think suggested. "You've worked hard all your life and you should be able to relax in retirement. You've earned it. It's a vacation."

"In your case," Didja Hear told Fast Talkin', "your life was one long vacation and you should start workin' like crazy to make up for it."

I Think took another sip of his drink. "I fear my time is coming, and death is at the door."

"Can you be a little more upbeat?" Listener pleaded. "You're driving away customers!"

"I can't help it, Listener. I worry about what's going to happen to humanity. There is much that is good in our society, but there are also wars, famine and dictators like Big Feet. ... By the way, I can't pay for the drink."

"That figures. If there's anything that's tough to take it's a deadbeat with a worldview."

"My time is coming, Listener. I do not dread death. Death comes to us all."

"I've been wondering why it doesn't take Big Feet."

"You have a good point, Listener. I have wondered about that myself. Maybe Big Feet is the exception to the rule. But, alas, I won't be around to see if it is true." He got off his bar stool. "Farewell, Listener. Any parting thoughts?"

"You still owe me two hopeks for the drink."

I Think headed for the exit.

"And take care my friend. I will miss you."

The next day I Think began the task of arranging all the stone slabs (and old beer cans) near the writings he had made on the wall of the cave. He piled them neatly, hoping that someday later generations would find his records. This was his description of life in Bethlehem and Utter Bliss at the time he lived.

After completing this task, I Think continued his cheerful but tiring final days. Every moment he spent with his children and grandchildren and friends was special to him.

And when I Think died, on a cool, clear winter day, there was a smile on his face. His family and friends mourned. Listener closed his saloon for a day, and Emperor Big Feet, then in his seventies, ordered twenty-three minutes of mourning. Big Feet had not entirely lost his sense of humor—that was one minute for every vote I Think had received in the election.